This book is ded'---' ·
between them r

Special thanks t
who designed th
Gustavo Garramu   ... .ith's
suggestions and euits were helpful and much
appreciated. Without their support and talents,
Spenser's Story would not have been told.

Spenser's Story of the Constitution

ISBN-13: 978-0692760994 (Ozymandias Press)
ISBN-10: 0692760997 Printed in U.S.A

The map of Philadelphia seen in this book is based
on a 1986 map created by James Terrio, courtesy of
Friends of Independence National Historical Park.

The typeface used with many of the illustrations and
the Constitution is called American Scribe, and was
created from the penmanship of Timothy Matlack.
Matlack engrossed the Declaration of Independence
after the first draft was penned by Thomas Jefferson.
The original Constitution of the United States was penned
by Jacob Shallus, a Pennsylvania General Assembly clerk.

Publishing Co

www.OzymandiasPublishing.com

We welcome your feedback at
feedback@OzymandiasPublishing.com

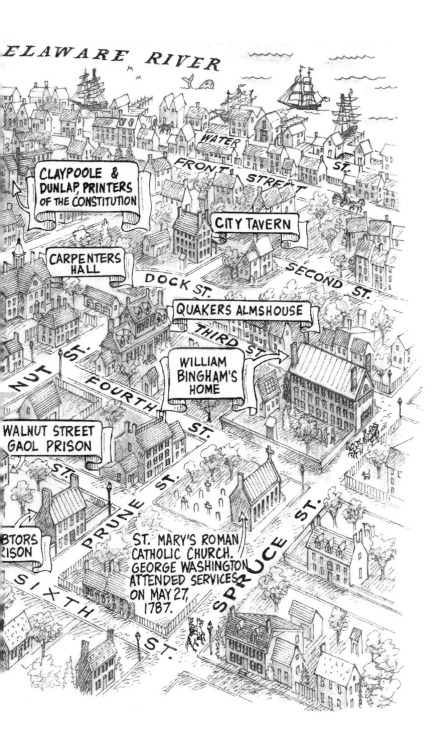

" .....when a housefly flaps his wings, a breeze goes round the world; when a speck of dust falls to the ground, the entire planet weighs a little more; and when you stamp your foot, the earth moves slightly off its course. Whenever you laugh, gladness spreads like the ripples in a pond; and whenever you're sad, no one anywhere can be really happy. And it's much the same thing with knowledge, for whenever you learn something new, the whole world becomes that much richer. "

The Phantom Tollbooth
by Norton Juster
Random House, 1964

Editor's Preface

From time to time I travel to Philadelphia. Occasionally during these trips I browse through one or another of the city's fine old antique shops.

Because I cannot afford to buy much, these trips are usually just an opportunity to appreciate the fine craftsmanship of earlier times.

Recently, however, in a shop near the corner of Second and Chestnut Streets, I found a musty old trunk. The proprietor said she had come upon it just days before; she planned to have it opened and restored soon.

But, she said that if I would purchase it "as is" perhaps I could save some money and she some time and trouble. A deal was made and I left with my modest treasure.

Later, when I pried open the rusted lock, I discovered the trunk was not empty. Deep in a corner was a thick sheaf of old, stained papers tied in an embroidered ribbon.

For the next several days I tenderly read the old pages. The papers were a unique diary in nine parts, each part a separate story.

One part in particular aroused my interest and spurred me to spend several months' online checking facts.

I found that the stories were remarkably accurate from a historical perspective. So I called several scholars to see if the author's existence could be verified.

I was astonished to hear them say that "an unusually large, black cat" named Spenser had in fact been the Caretaker of the State House in Philadelphia during much of the late-18th Century.

"Ben Franklin," said one, "clearly cited such a cat in a charming letter to his grandson William in 1789. 'Spenser,' said Franklin in the letter, 'joined me for dinner last evening and we enjoyed a robust discussion of the Grand Convention of two years past.' "

Another scholar noted that Robert Morris, during his stay at the local debtors' prison, often remarked to visitors of the "delicious apples and other fruit brought me by my old friend Spenser."

Now, having checked the historical facts and proofs of the author's existence, I came to my last big questions: Could a cat talk? Could he write?

Easily answered......of course he could. Literature abounds with examples. Did not Eeyore and Piglet and the Pooh speak regularly with Christopher Robin? What of Wilbur and Charlotte talking openly with Fern? And the dog Tock with Milo?

Cats and crickets, dogs and mice, elephants and crabs—all have been recorded. In fact, an expert in animal behavioralism told me that writing and talking animals were so common now that its probability was beyond the statistical margin of error.

And so, having satisfied myself that Spenser's story is accurate and true, I now offer it to you, the reader.

Spenser's Letter to his Daughter

My Dear Cassie,

As I write this to you I am nearing the end of my ninth illustrious life. I have been fortunate during my lives to be present at a number of events that have become part of history.

I have counted among my friends famous explorers, statesmen, athletes. inventors and military leaders. And, I must add with all humility, I have been of substantial assistance to many of them. In truth, the healthy state of our beloved country today would have been much reduced had I not been available to help where so often needed.

Yet, I am a cat before my time. No biographer has stepped forward to tell my story or to record my important roles in history. I worry that after I am gone what I know to be the real truth will never be told.

I urge you to pay particular attention to the journal that recounts the creation of our nation through the writing and signing of the United States Constitution.
It was the single most important enterprise my colleagues and I ever undertook... and the most difficult.

General Washington, old Ben Franklin, the brilliant Alexander Hamilton, James Madison, Robt. Morris, Chas. Pinckney, Mason and Randolph were all there. I can still remember the long and heated debates they had. It took them four months to finally agree. But when they did they had changed history.

Unfortunately, very few people know much about it any longer. Some lawyers, some teachers, a few scholars--that's about all. Perhaps, one day, you can tell my story of the Constitution, and the men and cat who wrote it. My place in history, Cassie, rests on your reliable haunches.

With all my love, I remain:

Your devoted father,

Spenser

I Meet with Ben Franklin

The winter of 1787 was particularly cold. Bitter winds swirled up Chestnut Street from the river nearby, and ice and blown snow made gazing from my bedroom window nearly impossible.

It was February in Philadelphia and I was preparing to join my old friend Ben Franklin for dinner. Earlier that day I had received by messenger Ben's short note.

Franklin

"Spenser," he wrote, "will you join me tonight for a warm drink. I have learned today that our work with the 13 states is not yet finished. Please join me at eight o'clock."

As Ben lived only a few blocks away
I was not overly concerned with the
ill-weather. I would not need my carriage;
I could walk to Ben's house. Nor was
it required that I get all dressed up;
Ben was not noted for his fancy clothes.
In fact, he no longer wore a wig and
never powdered his hair.

While I generally agreed with him
on most matters, I was known to cut
a dashing figure and took more care
of my attire than did Ben.

This particular evening I selected
a waistcoat with a high, stand-up
collar with silver buttons at the
sleeves and pockets. My breeches
were high-waisted and long over the
knees. The vertical-striped stockings
led to my much-pointed shoes with
quite large, round silver buckles.

My vest, of course, was made
of rich, red velvet.

Earlier in the day I had purchased
at the apothecary shop a bottle of Ben's
favourite gout remedy—Turlington's
Balsam. The winters were particularly

hard on Ben, his gout and kidney stones causing clear discomfort and making it difficult for him to get around much. He rarely left his home any more, but preferred to have guests join him by his hearth.

All this is not to say that Ben was not active in his retirement years. Although he was now 81 years old, he served as Governor of Pennsylvania, and also was supervising a three-story addition to his house. He was President of the American Philosophical Society, was helping his grandson build a print shop and he managed two properties on High Street.

Dr. Benjamin Franklin was, quite simply, one of the most respected men in all the states. For Ben to have proposed a meeting on such short notice meant that he had something important to discuss with me. I should not be late.

The walk from the State House on Chestnut Street where I lived to Ben's home off High Street* was only

---

*Editor's note: High Street has since been renamed Market Street.

about three blocks. I arrived at Ben's punctually at eight o'clock and was met at the door by his charming daughter Sally.

"Welcome to our home, Spenser, on this bitter, cold night. I trust you had no misstep on your walk over, and that your family is well," she said. "Please do come in out of the cold."

"We are all quite well, thank you Sally," I replied, stepping into the warm, candle-lit foyer.

"Father," she said, "received a letter from Mr. Hamilton in New York this morning. After writing to you he has been in his study ever since. I'm sure it's a matter of great urgency."

She took my walking stick, helped me off with my heavy overcoat and escorted me down the center hall to Ben's study.

The scene on entering was a familiar one. Ben was seated behind his oak desk, peering intently at a large, wrinkled map spread out before him. All the four walls, save before two windows and a fireplace, were covered floor to ceiling with books.

Other books and papers lay everywhere around the room.

In one corner, on a round table, lay a fireman's helmet, haphazardly surrounded by still more books and papers. Drawings of the proposed addition to his house were pinned to the framework around one of the windows. A walking stick served as a paperweight for one side of his map, while a checkerboard held the other half in place.

"Good evening, Ben," I said.

He seemed not to hear, and his head and large shoulders remained bent over the map.

"It is good to see you, Ben," I said, somewhat louder.

"The problem rests with the states," he said, still looking at his map. "Always has."

He finally lifted his head and looked directly at me. "Forgive me old friend," he apologized, "I should welcome you before I discuss business."

As I've mentioned, Ben wore no wig.
Instead he let his long, greying hair
fall nearly to his shoulders. A large,
round man he wore a brown jacket
and tight-fitting vest, with short ruffles
at the neck and cuffs. His clear grey eyes
smiled at me from beneath his bifocals.

"I have brought you," I said, "a new
bottle of Turlington's for your gout.

It appears, however, that you are in fine health."

Ben had left his chair and had moved from behind his desk to greet me. Once the formalities were over, and we were both seated, he got right to business.

"I have heard from Alexander Hamilton," he said, "that the Continental Congress in New York has issued a call for a special Convention to revise the Articles of Confederation. It is an opportunity, Spenser, that we cannot afford to miss. If our nation is to grow strong we must act now to unify the states. We cannot survive if we remain 13 quarrelling, selfish and independent states."

His words took me back several years to when I was a young cat just beginning a job as caretaker at the State House. At the time—on July 4, 1776 to be exact—the colonies declared their independence from Great Britain and the taxing rule of King George III.

It was Thomas Jefferson of Virginia who had written this Declaration of Independence. Fifty-five patriots from the 13 colonies had signed it. It was the official declaration of war with Great Britain, and it had been written and signed at my State House. In fact, it was during these deliberations that I had first met Ben Franklin. Despite my youth, being barely older than a kitten, I had been able to assist Mr. Jefferson with some matters of wording. Ben had heard of my help, and we have remained close friends ever since.

The Declaration of Independence, as you will remember, led to the great War of Independence, the Revolutionary War some called it. The War lasted seven years. It was a long, hard and bloody affair, and we all lost many dear friends and family. But, at its end we had finally won our liberty and the states' freedom from foreign tyranny.

When it was over our soldiers were tired and poor, many had been away from their families, homes and farms for several years. They had won their freedom, but they had sacrificed dearly to do so. After the War they returned to their homes in Massachusetts and Connecticut, Virginia and Georgia, Pennsylvania and North Carolina. They were ready to return to their families and get back to work.

They left the political leaders in the states to form a new government to take the place of the despised British King. But because the King had been a selfish and unfair ruler, these new leaders of a new country did not want another King. They did not want a strong government telling them what to do. They did not want most of their money taken from them in taxes. So when they created the new government they made it weak and powerless. They did not let it tax the people. Without any money the new government could not do much.

While this seemed a good idea at the time, it didn't work for very long. By 1787, just a few years after the War, the states were hopelessly arguing and squabbling with each other.

The farmers who had fought in the War were still very poor and many had lost their farms. The state leaders did nothing to help. They no longer worked together, as they did during the War, and each state went in its own direction with its own government. The Continental Congress, which was supposed to be the government of all the states, was too weak and poor to do anything.

Something had to be done or soon the United States would split apart. Instead of one strong country there would be 13 weak, little countries. Many leaders, some in almost every state, did not want this to happen.

Ben Franklin was one of these men who wanted one country, not 13. His voice now startled me out of my thoughts.

"Spenser, are you okay?" he asked. "You seem not to be listening to me at all."

"Quite to the contrary," I replied, "I have heard everything you've had to say—for years now."

"I see," he said, smiling at me.

"Well, the Federal Convention will be held at the State House and will begin on May 14. That does not leave you very much time to prepare. I expect that we will see again many old friends.
Mr. Hamilton hopes to come from New York, and General Washington should attend from Virginia with that bright young man James Madison. It should make for an interesting summer here."

I could not tell Ben that I had not heard much of what he said. But I had heard enough to know that in the spring, less than three months away, a Grand Convention would be held at my State House. And I knew that on the results of this meeting would rest the future of our beloved country—for better or for worse.

I Prepare for the Convention

It was not long after I had met with Ben Franklin that the news arrived in Philadelphia of the farmers' rebellion in Massachusetts. By the time we heard of it the fighting was over and the farmers had been defeated. But the armed uprising scared many leaders in all the states.

As I have mentioned, after the War the men who had fought for our independence went home to their farms, shops and families. But business was not good after the War, and people in one state could not buy goods and crops from workers in another state unless they paid a heavy tax.

The State House.

Farmers, who grew wheat, tobacco, cotton, corn or fruit, could not sell their crops for very much money, and so they went into debt. They borrowed money to keep their farms going. When they could not pay back the money they owned to banks and other lenders, their farms were taken from them and sold. Sometimes the farmers were put in jail, or were sold to wealthy people as servants.

In western Massachusetts the farmers were particularly poor and most were deep in debt. When they could not pay their taxes they asked the state government to help them. When the state did not help them, the angry farmers became a mob and threatened the local judges and courts. They thought that if they frightened the judges they would not be able to meet and take away the farmers' land and homes.

The leader of this mob was Daniel Shays. When Shays and his followers—called pitchfork patriots—armed themselves with guns, and threatened to start another war, the government called out its troops and overcame the mob by force.

But Shays' Rebellion, as it was called, deeply frightened the government leaders. These leaders, like General George Washington of Virginia, realized that the states would continue to bicker and fight unless they created a stronger national government.

Shays' Rebellion, however, was only one reason many leaders wanted to hold a meeting in Philadelphia. On almost any street corner, and in the markets and taverns, people were talking and arguing about the weakness of the states and the threat to us from other countries.

The large, clean, covered market on High Street, which was open for business every Wednesday and Saturday morning, was a particularly good place to hear news from other states. While people bought fish, fresh caught from the Schuylkill and Delaware Rivers nearby, or meat, butter, vegetables and fruits, they talked.

One morning I overheard a traveller from North Carolina telling a fur trader from Pennsylvania how lucky he was.

"My brother lives in western territory called Tennessee," the traveller from the south said. "It is across the Appalachian mountains from me. He is a hard-working farmer, and has cleared a fine spread. But he cannot take his crops across the mountains because they are too high and have no roads. And he cannot take his crops west to the Mississippi River, so they can be moved by ship and sold in Georgia or South Carolina, because Spain controls the river and will not let him use it unless he pays heavy taxes or bribes.

"Our state is not strong enough," he continued, "to make Spain leave. And, to tell the truth, our Confederation Congress cannot help either. It is too weak, and has no army or navy to fight the Spanish. My brother is barely getting by, and he cannot afford to buy shoes for his two sons and daughter."

The frontiersman listened, and when the North Carolina man was finished talking, he finally spoke.

"I also have a story to tell," he said. "I am a trader in furs and pelts. As you can see, even my clothes are made from buckskins. I spend many months every year in the woods in the Northwest Territory west of New York and Pennsylvania trapping and trading with Indians for furs and skins. I like my life, and I work hard to make my living.

"But the British, not the Spanish,
are the ones that make my job difficult.
King George has left many of his soldiers
in their forts to the north and west.

These British trade with the Indians for furs, and then ship them to England. While this hurts my business, and I must spend more time to make a living, I am even more upset with our own government.

"It is too weak to make the British leave, even though we won the War. I think it is insulting to our country that British soldiers and traders remain on our land. Our legislature is a laughingstock, a joke. They rarely meet because almost nobody comes. And when they do meet, in New York, they never do anything because it only takes a few states to say no."

"You're right," the other traveller said, "and the states don't care either. They are too busy arguing among themselves. They argue over who owns what land, and which states control the traffic of ships on rivers. Some of the leaders in the states don't want a strong national government because they are afraid of having another king. They think we will lose our freedoms and liberty if there is a strong national government that has more power than the individual states."

"But people like us," said the other man, "are being hurt by all this bickering and arguing between states. Many of us have less money than we did when King George III ruled us. Heaven knows, I don't want another King. And I will never give up my freedoms. But, something has to change. Something must be done soon."

At the time of this marketplace discussion these men did not know that in only a few months a convention would be held in Philadelphia to discuss how to make the government stronger and better. They did not know that barely two blocks from where they stood 55 leaders from 12 of the 13 states would meet to try to solve these problems.

Because I was very busy preparing for this convention I hurried on to do my shopping. My wife Stephanie had given me a long list of groceries to pick up for dinner.

She had said to look closely at the beans and peas and judge which I thought looked better. The sugar peas seemed to me more firm, so I chose them over the beans. Because Stephanie had planned a leg of pork, which two days earlier had been stuffed with sausage meat and corn, I selected several herbs which I've always found useful in cookery. I bought some sage, which of course only goes well with pork or cheese. Also, I picked up some sweet thyme and parsley.

I bought the yellowest bell peppers I could find, several apples, a sampling of Malaga grapes, and a number of potatoes. Dessert, due to be one of Stephanie's best rice puddings, required only that I pick up a quarter-pound of rice, milk, a stick of cinnamon, a dozen eggs and some butter. I could taste it already.

Walking home through the cobblestone streets of Philadelphia was always a pleasure for me. Young children, often in the park behind the State House, played hopscotch, jumped rope or flew kites.

They would recover hoops from old barrels and roll them through the streets or along the brick or wood sidewalks.

Small shops were everywhere, painted in bright colors—red, blue, green, and yellow. Carefully lettered signs hung outside identifying the merchants inside as wig makers or boot makers, blacksmiths or gunsmiths, weavers or pewter workers.

Philadelphia was the largest and most modern city in the country. Nearly 40,000 people lived in and around the city, and it was a thriving port where ships unloaded their goods from around the world. There are several great brick homes on estates a full city block in size, with their own gardens and stables.

Because Philadelphia was a big city, and had more schools and private tutors available for the children than most cities and towns, many children there learned to read. When they had finished their chores, which took much of their time, they often read.

Sometimes, when they could buy or borrow a copy, they read <u>Little Pretty Pocket Books</u> from England. *Mother Goose's Melody* and *Goody Two-Shoes* were two favourites.

Although Philadelphia was the most modern, up-to-date city in America, it had its problems too. Flies and mosquitoes were everywhere because people threw their slops and left-over food in the streets. Dead animals sometimes were left to decay in the streets, and in some areas open sewers caused quite a stink. Tanning shops, breweries and stables added to the smells that were carried throughout the city by the frequent breezes off the river.

Shackled prisoners from the Walnut Street jail would regularly try to clean the streets and outdoor privies. They were named after their carts—'wheelbarrow men.' But it was difficult for them to keep up with the smelly refuse.

The city also was known for its bells. Church bells rang on Sunday announcing worship services. And, several evenings each week, evening bells announced the next morning's market. Peddlers selling their wares rang hand bells along streets in the mornings.

At night, watchmen called out the time and weather every hour till dawn. Tavern patrons, in particular, found this helpful.

The people of Philadelphia came from almost everywhere in the world. Many of the farmers who lived around the city were from Germany, or were descended from Dutch or German settlers. The sailors who sailed into the city's busy port were from all over the world and spoke many languages. Rugged frontiersmen, Indians, and Quakers in their black garb and broad hats mixed with wealthy travellers from France, Great Britain and other European countries.

Transportation was by foot, by horse, by stagecoach or carriage. The loud, sharp sounds of horse hoofs and carriage wheels on the cobblestone streets were common from dawn until after dark. Visitors from the quiet countryside often found sleeping difficult in the noisy city night.

When I finally got home that afternoon I had missed lunch, which Stephanie always served precisely at 11:00 am. My wife was firm on maintaining regular hours for meals. Breakfast was at 7:00 am. sharp, with dinner at 4:00 pm. and a light supper or snack at 10 o'clock in the evening.

I gave Stephanie the groceries, along with a little nuzzle on the cheek. She would need most of the next four hours to prepare for dinner. With eight children still living at home, and stop-ins by our other 12 children and their families not uncommon, Stephanie spent a good bit of time each day in the kitchen.

After changing into some work clothes I began my afternoon rounds of the State House. With the Federal Convention now only a few weeks away, there was still much work to do.

My daughters Mary and Theresa worked with their mother on the meals, and also helped with washing the family's clothes. Sons Ezra and Duncan were on rat patrol in the main building. With so much garbage and trash in the city streets it was a full-time job to keep rats out of the State House. It just would not do to have rats and mice underfoot when the delegates arrived.

Mathew, Mark, Luke and John— our older sons still at home—were busy washing windows, painting walls and ceilings, repairing loose and cracked bricks, scrubbing floors, polishing brass fixtures, replacing candles and generally cleaning up everywhere on the grounds around the building.

The State House, where the Federal Convention would be held and where we lived, was about 50 years old. It had served as the meeting place of the Pennsylvania legislature and the local court for many years.

However, it was already the most historic and best-known building in the 13 states. In 1775, just 12 years earlier, General George Washington had been appointed Commander-in-Chief of the Continental Army in the State House.

In 1776 at the State House the Declaration of Independence was signed and adopted. Five years later, in 1781,

the Articles of Confederation,
the new nation's first laws, were signed.
For most of eight years during the
Revolutionary War, between 1775
and 1783, the Second Continental
Congress had met in the State House.

During all this time I had been working
at the State House*. I started as the
caretaker in the early 1770s. My family
lived in a small wing to the west of the
main building. Our home, while not
roomy for a family as large as mine,
was comfortable.

With the State House at the
center of so many important events
and meetings over the past 15 years,
my circle of old friends was wide.
Thomas Jefferson, John Adams,
Patrick Henry, Ben Franklin, General
Washington and many others were all
dear friends. Several of them would
be at the Federal Convention in May.
I looked forward to seeing them again.

---

*Editor's note: The State House was later renamed
Independence Hall because both the Declaration
of Independence and the U.S. Constitution
were signed there.

The Delegates Arrive

№ 3

May finally came, as it always does, and we awaited the arrival of the delegates. The State House, I must say, had never looked better. In the large Assembly Room where the Convention was to take place I had desks and chairs, inkwells, quill pens and candles ready, if necessary, for as many as 60 people.

The state legislatures, who appointed most of the delegates from their states, had named 74 men as delegates. Over the course of the meeting only 55 of them would attend at one time or another. Some came and left for personal or political reasons; others arrived late. Some came on time and stayed throughout the Convention.

On an average day there were around 30 delegates present. I never needed all my desks or chairs.

In Philadelphia there was an undercurrent of excitement and anticipation. Rumors were widespread that this Convention would discard entirely the weak Articles of Confederation, which currently served us, and write a whole new Constitution. This was not what the meeting had been called to do. It was only supposed to revise the Articles where needed in order to make them better able to govern the 13 states.

Already, by early May, several delegates from Virginia had arrived. Most of the Pennsylvania delegates lived in Philadelphia and were present.

Ben Franklin and I had talked many times that spring and he had told me that my old friend Patrick Henry from Virginia had been selected to attend but decided not to come. Mr. Henry refused to come because, in his words, he "smelt a rat." Ben had joked that with me at the State

House that would not be a problem—
I would see to it that there were no
rats around.

Of course, what Mr. Henry meant was
that he thought the Convention would
establish a strong national government
that would threaten the hard-earned
rights and freedom of the individual
states. Like many others he did not
want to be part of that.

Patrick Henry, along with others
including Sam Adams of Massachusetts
and Governor George Clinton of New
York, were not in favour of a strong
national government. They believed that
a federal government with powers to
tax, print money and establish a national
Supreme Court would swallow up the
states and their rights. Men like Patrick
Henry and Governor Clinton were called
"Anti-Federalists." They did not support
a strong 'Federal' government. They were
happy with the 13 states running their
own affairs, with no central government
telling them what to do. The state of
Rhode Island, in fact, believed this so

much that they never did come to the Convention. Only 12 states sent delegates.

For a while it looked like other states, in addition to Rhode Island, would not come. States like Connecticut and Maryland balked at attending. But that changed when George Washington said he would attend.

General Washington was the most respected, admired and best-liked man in the whole country. He had led the Continental Army for seven years during the Revolutionary War. He was a hero, and when the war ended he had left the Army and returned to his home, Mt. Vernon in Virginia. Some people had asked him to take over the government; a few even wanted him to become King.

But Washington did not seek fame for himself. He did not need to hold on to power after his leadership of the army during the war was finished.

He had been a true servant to his country, and wanted no personal rewards in return.

Yet George Washington cared deeply about his new country. And, like many others, he believed that the United States was weak, that if something were not changed soon the 13 states would split further apart and there would be more fighting—this time possibly between states. He remembered Shays' Rebellion in Massachusetts, and wanted to prevent more revolts in the future.

When Virginia asked him to go to the Philadelphia Convention he reluctantly said yes. He would have preferred to stay with his family, but he did not. Once again, his country needed him.

George Washington arrived in Philadelphia on May 13, the day before the Convention was due to begin. It had taken him four days of travel by horseback and carriage to make the trip from his Virginia home on the Potomac River. When he arrived outside Philadelphia dozens of friends were there to meet him. They escorted him through cheering crowds into the city.

The Philadelphia City Cavalry led
the way dressed in their white breeches,
high black boots and round hats bound
with silver. Cannons and rifles were fired
in salute. Flags were waved everywhere,
and ringing church bells filled the air.

General Washington was escorted to Mrs. House's Boarding House where he planned to stay during the Convention.

But for Robert Morris, one of the richest men in Philadelphia, that would not do. His old friend General Washington must stay at his home with his family. Robert Morris, who also was a delegate to the Convention, had served General Washington during the Revolutionary War raising money for the Army. They had become good friends during the war, and General Washington accepted Morris's invitation.

Morris

Unfortunately, Morris later lost all his money and was put in debtor's prison for several years. But that was not until later. For now Robert Morris's home was one of the largest and most beautiful in the city.

It was also conveniently located, only a few blocks from both the State House and Ben Franklin's house. In fact, General

Washington spent that first evening in Philadelphia at Dr. Franklin's talking about the war, the problems in the country, and the Federal Convention which was scheduled to start the next day.

However, the Convention did not start the next day. There were not enough states or delegates present to begin. In order for the Convention to get underway more than half the states had to be present. That meant that it could not begin until at least seven of the 13 states (called a quorum) were there.

On Monday, May 15, only two states were there—Pennsylvania and Virginia. Why? First, because the weather that spring had been rainy, and the roads were little more than paths of mud. Carriages and stagecoaches simply could not make good time in the deep mud.

Also, many delegates had long distances to travel. Those traveling from Georgia or South Carolina were faced with a two-week journey if they came by boat, and more if they travelled by land.

The biggest reason many delegates were not there on time, however, was simply that time was not very important. People in 1787 did not pay much attention to plans or schedules. They would get there when they got there. And that was that.

It would be two more weeks before the Federal Convention finally got underway. The missed time, however, did not go to waste—not by a long shot. Each morning the delegates from Virginia met to discuss plans for the Convention. They met at the Indian Queen Tavern, where several of them also had rented rooms on the second and third floors.

Many Philadelphians thought the Indian Queen was the best tavern in the city. It had reasonable rates, numerous guest rooms, meeting rooms that could hold 80-100 people, sheds for guest carriages and stables for up to 83 horses. Other establishments, such as the City Tavern on Second Street, were highly regarded and attended, but not as large or elegant.

These daily meetings of the Virginia delegation included several of the best-known men in the country. In addition to the occasional presence of George Washington—James Madison, Governor Edmund Randolph and George Mason of Gunston Hall also attended.

James Madison, who years later became the fourth President of the United States, and who many people called the "Father of the Constitution," was one of the most important men at the Convention. Madison was quite small

Madison

in size. One person described him as no bigger than "half a bar of soap." But he also was one of the best-educated and most intelligent men in the country on the subject of government and politics.

He had read a great deal about ancient Greece and Rome and about their ideas on government and liberty. He also knew what his contemporaries in France and England had to say about the best way of ruling countries, while maintaining the peoples' freedoms.

James Madison (his friends called him Jemmy) was a quiet leader at the Convention. He and his Virginia friends used this free time before the Convention well. They wrote a plan for the government that was entirely new, which appropriately came to be called the Virginia Plan when it was presented later to the Convention.

The Convention was to begin soon. But while the delegates waited for more states and delegates to arrive, they found much to do in Philadelphia.

As more delegates arrived groups would meet at the taverns for dinner and talk. Or they would go to operas and concerts. During the days they took country walks, shopped at the market, went fishing in the nearby Delaware River and read newspapers like the *Pennsylvania Gazette* or the *Pennsylvania Packet*, where advertisements could be found on the front page and the news of the week followed.

John Bartram had a popular Botanical Garden near the city with beautiful and exotic plants and flowers from all over the world. Nearby there was a live camel for viewing.

Many delegates wrote home often to their wives and children. They did not know how long the Convention would actually last, but they knew they would not see their families for a long time.

After two weeks passed there finally were enough states represented (seven) to start the Convention. On Friday, May 25, 1787, the Federal Convention began.

The Convention Begins

№ 4

By 10 o'clock in the morning most of the delegates had arrived at the State House for the first meeting. Each delegate had to show papers (credentials) proving he was officially appointed by his state to serve at the Convention.

Once the delegates were all in the Assembly Room they elected George Washington to be president of the Convention. This was a wise and important decision. With General Washington as the leader everybody knew that what the Convention did would be for the good of the country. He would not be the leader if the business was

Washington

not important, or if the process was not straight-forward, dignified and honest.

Next the delegates decided on the rules they would follow at their meetings. Two rules they made were particularly important.

First, the meetings and what happened at them would be secret. The delegates did not want anybody outside the Convention to know what was going on inside until they had finally agreed on what to do. They wanted delegates to be free to say what they really believed. They thought that delegates could compromise and change their minds better if people outside the Convention did not know what they had said before.

The delegates felt this secrecy to be so important that they directed me to have soldiers posted outside the building so that no one could overhear them. Also, because Ben Franklin liked to talk so much—to everybody—at least one of the younger delegates was usually with him when he went out to the taverns in the evening.

More than once they had to remind him not to talk about the Convention.

Only two individuals who were not official delegates were permitted in the meetings. One was Major William Jackson, who was elected secretary. His job was to keep written records of the Convention, and to keep track of the votes. Although Major Jackson did this, the best record of the Convention was kept by James Madison of Virginia. He sat every day at his desk and wrote down much of what the delegates said. People who study history are very appreciative of James Madison's careful, precise work.

I was the only other individual permitted inside. Although I never said a word during the meetings, and I sat quietly in a small Windsor chair in the back of the room by the doors, I played a very important role at the Convention.

For example, when horses and carriages passed the State House on the cobblestone streets outside the meeting room it made a terrible racket.

Often it was so noisy the delegates could not hear even though they kept the windows closed.

It was my idea to have gravel laid on top of the larger cobblestones to help muffle the noise. This proved a great help to the delegates and I was roundly complimented.

Also, as you will soon learn, I was able to quietly advise some of the delegates on what to do. While history does not record my advice, or even my presence at the Convention, the fact of my involvement remains.

The second rule made by the Convention delegates was that each state would have one vote, not each delegate. That meant that all the 12 states were equal at the Convention. It did not matter which state had more delegates present, and it did not matter whether a state was large or small. Also, it was determined that a decision would be made when one-half the states agreed.

Thus, it took a 'majority' of the states (one-half or more) to approve by vote any action or decision.

A 'large' state, of course, was one where a lot of people lived. The largest states in the country were Virginia, Pennsylvania and Massachusetts. A 'small' state had a smaller population— like Delaware and Connecticut, and was usually smaller in size too.

As it developed, the Convention often became a contest between small states and large states. The small states were worried that the larger states would always tell them what to do. They felt that if a strong, new national government was based only on population, then they would not be equal and the people who lived in their state would suffer. For many of the men at the Convention this 'small state-large state' debate became the most important issue of all.

When the Convention opened the following week Ben Franklin, who had been sick on the opening day, arrived on his famous sedan chair.

Because of his age and illnesses walking was not easy for Ben. He often was not able to walk from his home to the State House. So he devised a special carriage that would carry him from door to door without the bumpy ride of a horse carriage.

He put a chair on a small platform with two long poles. After Ben sat down in the chair, four strong men would pick him up and carry the poles, chair and Ben on their shoulders to the State House. The building's large front doors would be opened and Ben would be carried through them into the Assembly Room and to his desk. His sedan chair would then be stored to the rear and side of the large room.

The day after Ben first attended the Convention, the delegates were confronted with a big surprise. The handsome, young governor of Virginia, Edmund Randolph, presented to the Convention a plan for a brand, new national government. The plan was called the "Virginia Plan". It had been written by the delegates from Virginia when they had arrived early for the Convention. Probably much of the new plan was written by James Madison, although no one's ever said for certain.

Whoever actually wrote it, the plan presented that day changed forever the way our government works. Instead of a weak, powerless federal government the Virginia Plan designed a strong national government in which the states by themselves could not make all the important decisions.

The old, weak government under the Articles of Confederation would not be revised; it would be done away with. A whole new government would be established. If the delegates supported the Virginia Plan, or one like it, there would be a new Constitution—and a new nation.

Writing the Constitution

When Governor Randolph of Virginia presented his state's plan for a new national government it startled and surprised many of the other delegates.

Randolph

Most delegates thought they had come to Philadelphia simply to change and improve the old government under the Articles of Confederation. Governor Randolph's Virginia Plan would do much more than this—it would create a new federal government and do away completely with the old Articles.

Young Governor Randolph took over three hours to present his state's plan to the Convention. It included 15 parts (called Resolves) and would become the basis of our government.

The plan divided the national government into three branches. The first was the legislative branch, which would make the laws of the United States. It would have two chambers (House and Senate) and together they would come to be called the Congress. The members of the House of Representatives would be elected by the people in the states. The members in the Senate would be appointed by the members of the House of Representatives.

Both of these chambers would represent people, not states. This meant that the states with the most people—like Virginia, Pennsylvania and Massachusetts—would have more power and influence in the national government than the small states.

This scared small states like Delaware, Connecticut and Maryland. They thought that the large states would control the new government and not pay any attention to the small states.

Also, under this Virginia Plan, the strong national government could look at the laws in the 13 states and say they were illegal. Any state law, then, could be discarded (nullified) by the federal Congress. This frightened those Convention delegates who thought the state governments should be stronger than the national government.

In addition to creating a strong national legislature the Virginia Plan established an Executive (later called President) who could "veto" an action or law approved by the Congress. To veto means to overrule or stop something—in this case an action by the Congress. If the proposed President could do this—overrule Congress— he would have real power and strength.

Some delegates thought he would have too much power—that he would become a tyrant, or even a king. There was much discussion during the Convention about the power of the President.

The final major provision of the Plan was the creation of a system of federal courts that would take some of the power from the state courts. Arguments of law and trade between states would be decided by these new national courts.

James Madison reads the Virginia Plan

When all the proposals made by Governor Randolph and the Virginia Plan were added together the result was a strong commitment by the delegates to a balanced, three-part government that would be supreme over the states.

One of the strongest supporters of this proposed new national government was a delegate from Pennsylvania named Gouverneur Morris (Gouverneur was his name, not a title). The talkative, intelligent Morris had lost a leg in a carriage accident when he was young, but this had not stopped him from being one of the leaders of the Convention.

Morris

Toward the end of the Convention, still four months away at this point, Gouverneur Morris would write the final draft of the Constitution. He also would write the remarkable and well-known Preamble to the Constitution—

words so important that many American children would memorize them in school for generations.

But even a man as gifted and intelligent as Gouverneur Morris could be wrong sometimes. When the debate first began on the new Constitution, Morris thought only the rich and well-born should be permitted to vote. If everybody could vote, not just those who owned land, he thought there would be terrible corruption. Perhaps people would sell their vote for money, and then corrupt people would be elected to office. This worried Gouverneur Morris.

Fortunately, other delegates were wiser on this matter and land-ownership and wealth never became a voting requirement.

But discussion between delegates over this and many, many other important matters occurred every day during the Convention that summer in 1787. Nobody got everything they wanted in the final Constitution.

They all had to compromise—that is, give up something they wanted in exchange for something else they wanted even more. If the delegates had not been willing to do this—to compromise— there would not have been a Constitution and probably not a nation at all.

Despite this eventual willingness by the delegates to compromise, the Convention nearly failed because of the small state/large state controversy.

A few weeks after Virginia offered its plan to the delegates the small states got together and proposed a plan of their own. It was called the New Jersey Plan and was presented by William Patterson.

Patterson had been born in Ireland and had been brought to this country by his parents when he was still very young. His father was a merchant and tin manufacturer, but he became a lawyer.

Patterson

Patterson was a small man—only a little over five feet tall—modest in character and neat of dress. He was also a fine public speaker. After the Convention he was elected to the Senate, and later served New Jersey as governor.

The plan William Patterson presented basically continued the weak government as it existed under the Articles of Confederation, although Congress would have the right to collect taxes and to make trade laws between states. There would be one chamber in Congress, not two, and each state would be represented equally regardless of size. The members of Congress would be appointed by the states, and not elected by all of the people.

Also under Patterson's plan the Executive (President) would be elected by Congress, and there would be more than one Executive. Some delegates, like Edmund Randolph and George Mason of Virginia, thought there should be several presidents. Mason believed one president should come from the

South, one from the Middle states, and one from the North. It seemed to some that if there were only one President he would be too strong and might become a tyrant and take away freedoms. Mason thought that each different section of the country should have a president represent its people and interests. When the Convention later decided there would be only one President it was an important compromise.

The delegates talked about this new plan for three days. They argued whether the country really needed a strong national government, or whether the 13 states should rule themselves. They hotly debated whether all states should be equally represented in Congress, and how representatives in the national legislature (Congress) would be elected. Would they represent states or people?

Delegate James Wilson of Pennsylvania opposed the small-state New Jersey plan. Born in Scotland, Wilson came to America when he was 23 years old. He was a lawyer, and 11 years earlier had signed

the Declaration of Independence.
At the Convention he often stood and
spoke for the elderly Ben Franklin when
Ben wanted to make lengthy remarks.

James Wilson believed that there
should be a strong national government.
And he felt that this strong government
should serve "people", not "states".
During the debates he said that a
state with 10,000 people should not
have the same rights and
importance as a state
with 40,000 people.
Wilson thought that the
"people" should vote for
their government leaders,
and they should elect
their President*. He also
believed there should be
only one President, not two or three.

*Editor's note: At the time the Constitution was written only
white men could vote. Most of society at that time did not
consider women, slaves or Native Americans the equal of
'white men', so they could not vote. In 1869 with passage
of the 15th Amendment African American men earned the
vote. It took 50 more years before women were granted
the vote (suffrage) with approval of the 19th Amendment.

James Wilson was one of the delegates who voted against the New Jersey Plan. Another was Alexander Hamilton of New York.

Hamilton was one of the youngest and most brilliant men at the Convention. During the Revolutionary War he had been one of General Washington's top aides. He also had been a courageous leader of his soldiers in battle. Born on an island in the British West Indies, he had moved to New York while still a boy.

Hamilton

Hamilton believed more than any other delegate in a strong, centralized national government. Just days after Patterson had submitted the New Jersey Plan, Hamilton presented to the Convention his own proposal. He modelled his ideas on the system of government in Great Britain, which he felt was the best in the world. According to Hamilton the President should be elected for his whole life, and so

should the members of the Senate—
as long as their behaviour was good.

The states, according to Hamilton,
would no longer be states but simply
subdivisions of the national government.
The leaders of these subdivisions would
be appointed by the national government.

It took Hamilton nearly a full day
to explain his plan to the delegates.
When he was finished the delegates
were courteous, but not one person
at the Convention supported him.
As one Delaware delegate said,
Hamilton "is praised by all but
supported by no gentleman."

Hamilton's plan for a strong national
government was too extreme for the
delegates. It is likely that Hamilton
himself knew this. But he wanted the
Convention to know what he believed
even if the delegates did not agree
with him. As so often happened at the
Convention, Hamilton later was willing
to compromise, and he supported
a national government that was not
as strong as he would have liked.

Alexander Hamilton presents his plan

On June 19, the day following Alexander Hamilton's long speech, the Convention voted against the New Jersey Plan. Only three out of the 10 states present supported the small-state plan. One state, New Hampshire, had not yet arrived at the Convention because there was no money in the state treasury to pay for delegate expenses. New Hampshire's delegates did come later.

But later almost never came. Two of the three delegates from New York left the Convention never to return. They did not like what was happening. They liked the New Jersey Plan, and when it was defeated they believed that the Convention was heading toward writing a new Constitution that would establish a strong national government.

Throughout most of the first half of the Convention it was continually threatened with breaking up. Some of the delegates did not want to compromise, and they preferred that the Convention fail rather than give in. Fortunately most of the delegates realized how important their work was and decided to stay.

Perhaps it was my dear friend Ben Franklin who, with one of his many stories, persuaded some delegates not to leave. At about this time someone gave Ben a strange gift of a two-headed snake preserved in a jar. Ben was very pleased with his gift and showed the snake to many of the delegates.

As he showed them the snake he asked them what they thought would happen if, when the snake came to a tree, one head went one way and the other head went the other way around the tree. If neither head would change its mind or compromise, Ben said, the snake probably would die of thirst.

Although Ben never actually said, perhaps he meant by this story that, for the good of all, the delegates ought to get together and move in the same direction toward a new Constitution. Maybe he thought that one snake head represented the states' supporters and the other the strong-central-government backers, and if they didn't get together everybody would lose.

Whatever was in Ben's mind when he told the story, the truth is that by early July, six weeks after the Convention began in May, many delegates were ready to go home. Some, like the two delegates from New York, actually did. Others were preparing to, until a very important compromise saved the day, and the Constitution.

The most difficult issue to resolve at the Convention was the debate over how to elect members of Congress. The large states wanted the 'people' to elect members to both the Senate and the House of Representatives. They wanted membership in the two chambers based on population. The small states wanted the states to be equally represented in Congress regardless of size or population. Neither side would give in, and the Convention was perilously close to dissolving.

On the steamy-hot evening of June 22 I attended a benefit performance at the Opera House sponsored to help Americans held captive by Algerian pirates. I was joined by my friend Roger Sherman of Connecticut. After the entertainment was over we decided to stop by a local tavern for something cool to drink.

Sherman

Sherman was one of the most respected delegates at the Convention. Although he represented a small state, he very much wanted the Convention to succeed. He was not one of those delegates who, when they did not get their way, left the Convention and went home. He kept looking for compromises that wouldsatisfy the delegates and help create a new Constitution.

Roger Sherman was 66 years old, an older man at a Convention of young men. As Sherman was the father of a large family (15 children) we had much in common, and I had known him for more than a decade. Sherman had begun his professional career as an apprentice shoemaker in his father's shop. As he grew older he taught himself law and later became a judge in his home state. He also was a public servant and was elected mayor of the town of New Haven for many years. John Adams called him "honest as an angel".

After we were seated at a quiet table at the tavern I asked Sherman what he thought of the progress made at the Convention.

"I am deeply concerned", he replied,
"that we may never resolve this split
over the Congress. Spenser, I do not
foresee my colleagues in Pennsylvania
and Virginia ever supporting equal
representation of states in the Congress.
Nor do I see men like Luther Martin
of Maryland or Gunning Bedford of
Delaware favouring proportional
representation based on population."

"Surely," I said, "there is some way to compromise and satisfy both of these groups. After all, there are two parts of the Congress, and two different views on their makeup. Perhaps one chamber of Congress could satisfy one group's requirements, and the other chamber could meet the needs of the other group. I'm not exactly sure how this might work, but it may be an idea to think about."

Sherman sat still for several minutes, not moving so much as a finger. I considered that he might not have heard me. Then he finally said, very quietly, "It most certainly is, my friend. I believe you may have touched on a possible solution. Your idea makes sense. I shall have to give it more thought."

And that's exactly what Roger Sherman did. He developed, with the help of other delegates from Connecticut, the most important compromise at a Convention marked by compromise. At first it was called the "Connecticut Compromise"; later it became known as the "Great Compromise".

What it did was provide each state equal representation in the Senate Chamber. Little Delaware would have the same vote as a large state like Pennsylvania.

But in the other chamber—the House of Representatives—the number of members from each state would be determined by the number of people in the state. Thus in one branch of Congress the "people" were represented, and in the other the "states". The big states were happy with the way the House was to be made up, and the small states were pleased with the make-up of the Senate.

While there was something for both sides in the Great Compromise, both sides also would have to give up something. Neither side got everything they wanted.

At first they were not at all willing to make this compromise. Mostly it was the delegates who wanted a strong, national government who opposed the compromise. James Madison and other "nationalists" fought it fiercely.

Because of this opposition when the first vote on the compromise was taken it wound up tied.

The whole Convention did not want to keep arguing about the Connecticut plan so it established a small committee to talk more about it. Every state had one delegate on this committee. The committee was told to decide what they thought the Convention should do and then make a recommendation to the other delegates.

The committee debated the compromise for several days. Finally the committee members voted in favour of the plan proposed by Roger Sherman, and they recommended that the whole Convention approve it.

Before the delegates did this, however, they had to decide how they would count slaves. The Southern states, who had a lot of slaves working on plantations, wanted all these slaves to count when deciding how many members they could have in the House of Representatives. Remember, the number of members of the House was based on a state's population.

If slaves counted as population then southern states like South Carolina and Georgia would benefit. Northern states who had no slaves did not want slaves counted at all.

Once again they decided to compromise. The delegates decided that five slaves would count as three people. This decision was called the Three-Fifths Compromise.*

Finally, on July 16, the full Convention voted five states to four states in favour of the Great Compromise. After this vote most of the delegates stopped thinking about leaving the Convention. While the Convention had come very close to failing, now the delegates realized that there would be a new Constitution and a strong, new national government.

---

*Editor's note: This part of the Constitution was changed nearly a century later by "amendments" that outlawed slavery and gave the vote to all men, regardless of race. Women had to wait another 50 years until the Constitution was amended to guarantee their right to vote. James Madison, George Mason and many other delegates did not like slavery. But they believed that a fight over slavery at the Convention would result in its failure and prevent the formation of a Union.

Many difficult decisions, and several more compromises, lay ahead. But with the Great Compromise behind them, the delegates were sure that other matters could be worked out.

And they were worked out. The Convention lasted another two months, and many very important decisions were made by the delegates.

There were many debates on the President, perhaps the most important on how he should be elected. James Wilson of Pennsylvania, and some other delegates, believed he should be elected directly by the people. He wanted to leave states out of the election process.

The Virginia Plan had suggested that the President be elected by the Congress. That would have left the People out of the process.

These were just two of many ideas proposed by the delegates. Finally the Convention decided to have "electors" from each state choose the President. These electors could be chosen either by the vote of the people in the states or by vote of the members of the state legislatures, whichever the state wanted. Each of these electors would vote for two people. The person who got the most votes would be elected President. The candidate who finished in second place would be the Vice President.*

---

*Editor's note: This has since been changed. Now, because of the 12th Amendment to the Constitution, these electors vote for one person for President, and one person for Vice President. The candidate who finishes in second place for President is not elected Vice President.

If no one received a majority of the votes of the electors, then the members of the House of Representatives would select the President.*

The delegates also had to decide how many years the President, and also members of the Congress, would be elected.

---

*Editor's note: This has been done twice in our history. In 1801 Thomas Jefferson was chosen President over Aaron Burr, and in 1825 John Quincy Adams was picked by the House of Representatives over Andrew Jackson.

Some Convention delegates thought the President should be elected for life. Others thought he should be elected for six or seven years, but not be able to seek re-election. They decided to elect the President for four years, but he could run for office again. They also decided to elect House members for two years, and Senators for six years.

In addition to matters that directly related to government and politics, the Convention delegates also had to make some decisions that were economic and related more to business. For example, the northern states were concerned with trade from other countries. If there were no controls over other countries selling their products in the United States then the merchants and businessmen in the north were afraid that foreign merchants would sell their products for less money than Americans could. People would buy foreign goods and American merchants would lose money and many might go out of business.

Many of the businessmen in the southern states were farmers or planters. And much of what they produced-- crops like tobacco, rice and cotton-- was sold to other countries such as France or England. In order to grow and gather their crops they used slaves in their fields. They were afraid that the national government might stop the slave trade. If this happened, and they couldn't get any more slaves, they would not be able to grow as many crops and they would lose money.

Once again, the delegates decided to compromise. They agreed that the Congress could not stop the slave trade for 20 years in the 13 states—not until the year 1808. This pleased the southern states.

In exchange the Congress could not control trade with other countries and between the states. Congress would have to pass Navigation Acts for this purpose—laws that would regulate shipping. This would help protect the merchants in the north, and pleased the northern states.

One other very important decision made at the Convention was not a compromise, but rather shows what one person alone can accomplish. Charles Pinckney of South Carolina, only 29 years old, was one of the youngest delegates at the Convention. During the Revolutionary War he had been captured by the British. For nearly two years he was a prisoner of war. After the war ended he served in the Continental Congress that called for the Convention in Philadelphia.

Pickney

At the beginning of the Convention Pinckney had proposed his own plan for a strong central government. It was similar to the Virginia Plan I've talked about earlier. Because of this similarity the delegates spent little time discussing Pinckney's ideas. He was very disappointed, but he put aside his plan and supported the Virginia delegates.

As the Convention drew to its conclusion, however, Pinckney believed something important was missing.

Most states at the time of the Convention had laws that prohibited Catholics, Jews and members of some other religious groups from being elected to public office. These states required that everybody elected to an office, the state legislature for example, make an oath that they were not a Jew or a Catholic. If they were they could not serve in office.

Young Charles Pinckney thought it was wrong that a person could be excluded from public office because of his religion. Virtually by himself he persuaded the Convention to include in the Constitution a clause that there would be no religious test for office. Because of this people of all religious faiths and beliefs can be elected to and serve in public office.

Charles Pinckney's effort on behalf of religious toleration in the Constitution was one of the last decisions made by the Convention. Previous to this, on July 26, the Convention had named a Committee on Detail to write the Constitution. My friend from Philadelphia, James Wilson, had done much of the actual writing. While Wilson and other delegates were putting the document together the rest of the delegates took a 10-day vacation.

They came back on August 6 and spent the next month debating the 23 Articles (sections) Wilson and his colleagues had written. During this time the delegates made their final decisions on what would be in the new Constitution. Roger Sherman of Connecticut had said earlier, "When you are in a minority, talk; when you are in a majority, vote."

And that was exactly what the delegates did—they voted on numerous questions that they had been unable to decide before the great Connecticut Compromise.

When they had completed voting on September 10, and the new Constitution had been finished, they asked another small committee, called the Committee on Style, to write the final draft. The Convention named to this important committee five men—

William Samuel Johnson of Connecticut was the Chairman. Others on the committee were James Madison, Alexander Hamilton, Rufus King of Massachusetts and Gouverneur Morris.

While all of these men helped to write the Constitution, Gouverneur Morris wrote the most important words of all—the 52 words in the Preamble. The "Preamble" comes before the first Article (section) of the Constitution and explains why the Constitution was written and what it does.

Morris

*"**We the People** of the United States, in Order to form a more perfect Union, establish justice, insure domestic Tranquillity, provide for the common defence, promote the general Welfare, and secure the Blessings of Liberty to ourselves and our Posterity, do ordain and establish this Constitution for the United States of America."*
—The Preamble

Perhaps the most important words of all, in the entire Constitution, are the first three—*"We the People"*. For the first time in history the 'People' were the source of authority. The right to rule went from the people to the government. A king did not write this Constitution, and a king did not decide how the government would rule the people. And, although the 55 delegates who wrote the Constitution were sent to Philadelphia by the states, Gouverneur Morris did not write in the Preamble "*We the States*". He believed the Constitution was written by the people and for the people. He said so when he wrote "*We the People,*" and the delegates said so when they signed the Constitution.

On September 17, 1787, the delegates had finished their work. On the table before them lay a new Constitution. They were pleased with the job they had done during their four months in Philadelphia. They were rightfully proud of their achievement. They had created a new nation with a strong national government to run it. At the same time they had taken great care not to endanger their precious and hard-earned freedoms.

The delegates had been careful not to give too much power and authority to any one person or group of people. They accomplished this by putting "checks and balances" on the three branches (parts) of government. A check means that no branch—not the Congress, the President or the Supreme Court— would have the power to control the other branches. The powers of the three branches would be "balanced" and equal.

For example, the Congress can make a law, but the President has to agree to it and then sign it. If the President does not like the law, he can veto it (not sign it). Then the Congress has to get two-thirds of all its members in both the House and the Senate to vote for the law (instead of one-half). If two-thirds of the Congress still wants the law then it is passed and the President's veto is overridden (does not count).

Even after a law is passed by the Congress and signed by the President, it still might be thrown out by the Supreme Court. If the Supreme Court thinks that a law does not agree with what the Constitution says, then the Court can declare it "unconstitutional".

There are other checks and balances. The President is the commander in chief (leader) of the nation's armed forces. But he cannot decide to go to war with another country. It is the Congress that has the authority under the Constitution to declare war.

Also, the President can make important appointments to government—like choosing a new Justice (judge) for the Supreme Court—but the Senate must approve the President's top appointments.

The most important "check" of all, however, is the voting rights system written in the Constitution. Remember, the Convention delegates decided to have Senators serve in office for six years, Members of Congress for two years and the President for four years.

When these officials have completed their term in office they have to be elected again—by a vote of the "People". The voters might decide to make a change and elect a new person to office. It is the Constitution of the United States that guarantees, through this built-in system of checks and balances, that the 'People' control their government.

For a few delegates these checks on the power of government were not enough. They were concerned that the rights and freedoms of the People were not guaranteed by the Constitution, even with checks and balances. They wanted a Bill of Rights that would protect people's individual freedoms included in the Constitution. For example, they wanted the right to practice their own religion, and the freedoms of speech and press.

If you'll recall, Americans had fought a hard war with Great Britain in order to have their freedom, and to get away from the tyranny of King George III. They did not want to give up their new freedom to another powerful government.

Most of the delegates still in Philadelphia on this vital day, however, did support and sign the Constitution. Of the 42 delegates present, 39 signed the document. Only three--George Mason and Edmund Randolph of Virginia, and Elbridge Gerry of Massachusetts—did not sign their names on the Constitution.

As the delegates came to the front of the room and one-by-one wrote their names on the last page of the Constitution, Ben Franklin leaned toward the President's chair where George Washington had sat during the Convention. He pointed out to the delegates nearby that there was carved into the back of the chair a sun. He said that during the Convention he had not been able to tell whether that sun was rising or setting. "But now, at length," he told them, "I have the happiness to know that it is a rising and not a setting sun."

Ben Franklin knew that sun was rising over a new nation. The Union the Constitution created would not be perfect, but it would be "more perfect," as Gouverneur Morris had written.

The delegates had done their job well. They had written a Constitution for themselves and for generations to come. As James Wilson said during the Convention, "We should consider that we are providing a Constitution for future generations and not merely the circumstances of the moment."

Gouverneur Morris and James Wilson with General Washington, seated in the rising sun chair

But while the Convention had nowfinished its work and was ending, the delegates and their allies still had much to do before the Constitution was finally accepted.

In order for the Constitution to take effect the People had to vote for it. After all, it was their Constitution. The delegates had decided that nine of the 13 states had to ratify (vote for) the Constitution or it would not be approved. The People could still say no.

But they did not say no. Each state held a convention where people debated and argued about the Constitution. While some people opposed it and voted against it, a majority in every state firmly supported the Constitution. It was ratified in 1788.

In 1789, two years after the Federal Convention ended, and after it had been ratified (approved) by the states, the new nation's first government under the Constitution took office. General George Washington was elected President by a vote of the People through the electoral system established in the Constitution.

The First Congress was seated in the capital city of Philadelphia.* The first members of the Supreme Court were selected by President Washington and approved by the Senate. They took office in 1790.

In 1791, four years after the Constitution was written, a Bill of Rights was ratified by the states and added to the Constitution as the first 10 Amendments.

There are many wonderful and exciting stories about all those important events. But they will have to wait for another day. This evening I'm joining my old friend George Washington for dinner. The President has always valued my counsel.

---

*Editor's note: The nation's Capital was moved to Washington, D.C., in 1800. This was done to please states in the south that felt the capital should be located more centrally in the country, not in a northern state like Pennsylvania.

Editor's Postscript

It has been many years since I was a young student and was introduced by Mrs. Shoemaker, my 5th grade teacher, to civics and American history. Despite the years, I can still remember the excitement of my first Boston Tea Party, and my first trip across the dark, murky Charles River with Paul Revere, right under the guns of the British.

I gladly memorized Thomas Jefferson's famous words in the Declaration of Independence:

"We hold these Truths to be self-evident, that all Men are created equal, that they are endowed by their Creator with certain unalienable Rights, that among these are Life, Liberty, and the Pursuit of Happiness........"

I froze with General Washington's gallant men at Valley Forge.

But for the life of me I cannot remember much about the Constitution during school. Perhaps Mrs. Shoemaker and my other teachers taught me much about the Constitution and the extraordinary individuals who wrote it. More likely I was told by them how important this short document was to me and my friends—how it gave us our freedoms.

But they did not teach me much about the Constitution itself, and they didn't make it come to life. Perhaps they treated it like a dull, lifeless piece of paper that was just more words in our long history.

Or perhaps they thought I was too young to really understand the meaning of the words. The Constitution was better left for later when I would be older and better able to understand the "concepts" of government in the Constitution.

Or perhaps there was just too much history to teach and too little time available. Possibly an hour, or a day, about the United States Constitution was all the time they had.

It really does not matter anymore why it took me so long to learn about our nation's Constitution. What does matter is that you must learn about this amazing document and the people who wrote it. Spenser's tale is just the beginning of a much longer story—a story that has continued for more than 200 years.

The story of the United States Constitution started even before the Convention in Philadelphia in 1787. It will continue as long as people are free. And people will be free as long as they understand, preserve and protect their freedoms and system of government as contained in the Constitution. None of us, whether we are young or old, can afford to overlook the Constitution, or take it for granted. We cannot trust others to understand it for us. The Constitution is not like a lamp or a washing machine, we cannot hire someone else to fix it for us if it breaks down.

Our freedoms and our system of self-government, established for us in the Constitution, are too important to leave to someone else. If we do, then one day, surely as night follows day, the sun Ben Franklin noted on the back of General Washington's chair will be a setting and not a rising sun. We'll lose our hard-earned freedoms, and the story of the Constitution will end.
But if you understand the Constitution, and protect it, the story will never end.

Appendix

We the People

of the United States, in Order to form a more perfect Union, establish Justice, insure domestic Tranquility, provide for the common defence, promote the general Welfare, and secure the Blessings of Liberty to ourselves and our Posterity, do ordain and establish this Constitution for the United States of America.

Article. I.

Section. 1.

All legislative Powers herein granted shall be vested in a Congress of the United States, which shall consist of a Senate and House of Representatives.

Section. 2.

The House of Representatives shall be composed of Members chosen every second Year by the People of the several States, and the Electors in each State shall have the Qualifications requisite for Electors of the most numerous Branch of the State Legislature.

No Person shall be a Representative who shall not have attained to the Age of twenty five Years, and been seven Years a Citizen of the United States, and who shall not, when elected, be an Inhabitant of that State in which he shall be chosen.

Representatives and direct Taxes shall be apportioned among the several States which may be included within this Union, according to their respective Numbers, which shall be determined by adding to the whole Number of free Persons, including those bound to Service for a Term of Years, and excluding Indians not taxed, three fifths of all other Persons. The actual Enumeration shall be made within three Years after the first Meeting of the Congress of the United States, and within every subsequent Term of ten Years, in such Manner as they shall by Law direct. The Number of Representatives shall not exceed one for every thirty Thousand, but each State shall have at Least one Representative; and until such enumeration shall be made, the State of New Hampshire shall be entitled to chuse three, Massachusetts eight, Rhode-Island and Providence Plantations one, Connecticut five, New-York six, New Jersey four, Pennsylvania eight, Delaware one, Maryland six, Virginia ten, North Carolina five, South Carolina five, and Georgia three.

When vacancies happen in the Representation from any State, the Executive Authority thereof shall issue Writs of Election to fill such Vacancies.

The House of Representatives shall chuse their Speaker and other Officers; and shall have the sole Power of Impeachment.

Section. 3.

The Senate of the United States shall be composed of two Senators from each State, chosen by the Legislature thereof, for six Years; and each Senator shall have one Vote

Immediately after they shall be assembled in Consequence of the first Election, they shall be divided as equally as may be into three Classes. The Seats of the Senators of the first Class shall be vacated at the Expiration of the second Year, of the second Class at the Expiration of the fourth Year, and of the third Class at the Expiration of the sixth Year, so that one third may be chosen every second Year; and if Vacancies happen by Resignation, or otherwise, during the Recess of the Legislature of any State, the Executive thereof may make temporary Appointments until the next Meeting of the Legislature, which shall then fill such Vacancies.

No Person shall be a Senator who shall not have attained to the Age of thirty Years, and been nine Years a Citizen of the United States, and who shall not, when elected, be an Inhabitant of that State for which he shall be chosen.

The Vice President of the United States shall be President of the Senate, but shall have no Vote, unless they be equally divided.

The Senate shall chuse their other Officers, and also a President pro tempore, in the Absence of the Vice President, or when he shall exercise the Office of President of the United States.

The Senate shall have the sole Power to try all Impeachments. When sitting for that Purpose, they shall be on Oath or Affirmation. When the President of the United States is tried, the Chief Justice shall preside: And no Person shall be convicted without the Concurrence of two thirds of the Members present.

Judgment in Cases of Impeachment shall not extend further than to removal from Office, and disqualification to hold and enjoy any Office of honor, Trust or Profit under the United States: but the Party convicted shall nevertheless be liable and subject to Indictment, Trial, Judgment and Punishment, according to Law.

Section. 4.

The Times, Places and Manner of holding Elections for Senators and Representatives, shall be prescribed in each State by the Legislature thereof; but the Congress may at any time by Law make or alter such Regulations, except as to the Places of chusing Senators.

The Congress shall assemble at least once in every Year, and such Meeting shall be on the first Monday in December, unless they shall by Law appoint a different Day.

Section. 5.

Each House shall be the Judge of the Elections, Returns and Qualifications of its own Members, and a Majority of each shall constitute a Quorum to do Business; but a smaller Number may adjourn from day to day, and may be authorized to compel the Attendance of absent Members, in such Manner, and under such Penalties as each House may provide.

Each House may determine the Rules of its Proceedings, punish its Members for disorderly Behaviour, and, with the Concurrence of two thirds, expel a Member

Each House shall keep a Journal of its Proceedings, and from time to time publish the same, excepting such Parts as may in their Judgment require Secrecy;

and the Yeas and Nays of the Members
of either House on any question shall,
at the Desire of one fifth of those
Present, be entered on the Journal.

Neither House, during the Session of
Congress, shall, without the Consent of
the other, adjourn for more than three
days, nor to any other Place than that in
which the two Houses shall be sitting.

Section. 6.

The Senators and Representatives shall
receive a Compensation for their Services,
to be ascertained by Law, and paid out of
the Treasury of the United States. They
shall in all Cases, except Treason, Felony
and Breach of the Peace, be privileged from
Arrest during their Attendance at the Session
of their respective Houses, and in going to
and returning from the same; and for any
Speech or Debate in either House, they shall
not be questioned in any other Place.
No Senator or Representative shall, during
the Time for which he was elected, be
appointed to any civil Office under the
Authority of the United States, which shall
have been created, or the Emoluments
whereof shall have been encreased
during such time; and no Person holding
any Office under the United States,
shall be a Member of either House
during his Continuance in Office.

Section. 7.

All Bills for raising Revenue shall originate
in the House of Representatives; but
the Senate may propose or concur
with Amendments as on other Bills.

Every Bill which shall have passed the House
of Representatives and the Senate, shall,
before it become a Law, be presented to the
President of the United States; If he approve
he shall sign it, but if not he shall return it,
with his Objections to that House in which
it shall have originated, who shall enter
the Objections at large on their Journal,
and proceed to reconsider it. If after such
Reconsideration two thirds of that House
shall agree to pass the Bill, it shall be
sent, together with the Objections, to the
other House, by which it shall likewise be
reconsidered, and if approved by two thirds
of that House, it shall become a Law. But
in all such Cases the Votes of both Houses
shall be determined by yeas and Nays, and
the Names of the Persons voting for and
against the Bill shall be entered on the
Journal of each House respectively. If any
Bill shall not be returned by the President
within ten Days (Sundays excepted) after
it shall have been presented to him, the
Same shall be a Law, in like Manner as
if he had signed it, unless the Congress
by their Adjournment prevent its Return,
in which Case it shall not be a Law.

Every Order, Resolution, or Vote to which the Concurrence of the Senate and House of Representatives may be necessary (except on a question of Adjournment) shall be presented to the President of the United States; and before the Same shall take Effect, shall be approved by him, or being disapproved by him, shall be repassed by two thirds of the Senate and House of Representatives, according to the Rules and Limitations prescribed in the Case of a Bill.

Section. 8.

The Congress shall have Power To lay and collect Taxes, Duties, Imposts and Excises, to pay the Debts and provide for the common Defence and general Welfare of the United States; but all Duties, Imposts and Excises shall be uniform throughout the United States;

To borrow Money on the credit of the United States;

To regulate Commerce with foreign Nations, and among the several States, and with the Indian Tribes;

To establish an uniform Rule of Naturalization, and uniform Laws on the subject of Bankruptcies throughout the United States;

To coin Money, regulate the Value thereof, and of foreign Coin, and fix the Standard of Weights and Measures;

To provide for the Punishment of counterfeiting the Securities and current Coin of the United States;

To establish Post Offices and post Roads;

To promote the Progress of Science and useful Arts, by securing for limited Times to Authors and Inventors the exclusive Right to their respective Writings and Discoveries;

To constitute Tribunals inferior to the supreme Court;

To define and punish Piracies and Felonies committed on the high Seas, and Offences against the Law of Nations;

To declare War, grant Letters of Marque and Reprisal, and make Rules concerning Captures on Land and Water;

To raise and support Armies, but no Appropriation of Money to that Use shall be for a longer Term than two Years;

To provide and maintain a Navy;

To make Rules for the Government and Regulation of the land and naval Forces;

To provide for calling forth the Militia to execute the Laws of the Union, suppress Insurrections and repel Invasions;

To provide for organizing, arming, and disciplining, the Militia, and for governing such Part of them as may be employed in the Service of the United States, reserving to the States respectively, the Appointment of the Officers, and the Authority of training the Militia according to the discipline prescribed by Congress;

To exercise exclusive Legislation in all Cases whatsoever, over such District (not exceeding ten Miles square) as may, by Cession of particular States, and the Acceptance of Congress, become the Seat of the Government of the United States, and to exercise like Authority over all Places purchased by the Consent of the Legislature of the State in which the Same shall be, for the Erection of Forts, Magazines, Arsenals, dock-Yards, and other needful Buildings;—And

To make all Laws which shall be necessary and proper for carrying into Execution the foregoing Powers, and all other Powers vested by this Constitution in the Government of the United States, or in any Department or Officer thereof.

Section. 9.

The Migration or Importation of such Persons as any of the States now existing shall think proper to admit, shall not be prohibited by the Congress prior to the Year one thousand eight hundred and eight, but a Tax or duty may be imposed on such Importation, not exceeding ten dollars for each Person.

The Privilege of the Writ of Habeas Corpus shall not be suspended, unless when in Cases of Rebellion or Invasion the public Safety may require it.

No Bill of Attainder or ex post facto Law shall be passed.

No Capitation, or other direct, Tax shall be laid, unless in Proportion to the Census or enumeration herein before directed to be taken.

No Tax or Duty shall be laid on Articles exported from any State.

No Preference shall be given by any Regulation of Commerce or Revenue to the Ports of one State over those of another: nor shall Vessels bound to, or from, one State, be obliged to enter, clear, or pay Duties in another.

No Money shall be drawn from the Treasury, but in Consequence of Appropriations made by Law; and a regular Statement and Account of the Receipts and Expenditures of all public Money shall be published from time to time.

No Title of Nobility shall be granted by the United States: And no Person holding any Office of Profit or Trust under them, shall, without the Consent of the Congress, accept of any present, Emolument, Office, or Title, of any kind whatever, from any King, Prince, or foreign State.

Section. 10.

No State shall enter into any Treaty, Alliance, or Confederation; grant Letters of Marque and Reprisal; coin Money; emit Bills of Credit; make any Thing but gold and silver Coin a Tender in Payment of Debts; pass any Bill of Attainder, ex post facto Law, or Law impairing the Obligation of Contracts, or grant any Title of Nobility.

No State shall, without the Consent of the Congress, lay any Imposts or Duties on Imports or Exports, except what may be absolutely necessary for executing it's inspection Laws: and the net Produce of all Duties and Imposts, laid by any State on Imports or Exports, shall be for the Use of the Treasury of the United States; and all such Laws shall be subject to the Revision and Controul of the Congress.

No State shall, without the Consent of Congress, lay any Duty of Tonnage, keep Troops, or Ships of War in time of Peace, enter into any Agreement or Compact with another State, or with a foreign Power, or engage in War, unless actually invaded, or in such imminent Danger as will not admit of delay.

Article II.

Section 1.

The executive Power shall be vested in a
President of the United States of America.
He shall hold his Office during the
Term of four Years, and, together with
the Vice President, chosen for the
same Term, be elected, as follows

Each State shall appoint, in such Manner as
the Legislature thereof may direct, a Number
of Electors, equal to the whole Number of
Senators and Representatives to which the
State may be entitled in the Congress: but
no Senator or Representative, or Person
holding an Office of Trust or Profit under the
United States, shall be appointed an Elector

The Electors shall meet in their respective
States, and vote by Ballot for two Persons,
of whom one at least shall not be
an Inhabitant of the same State with
themselves. And they shall make a List of
all the Persons voted for, and of the Number
of Votes for each; which List they shall sign
and certify, and transmit sealed to the Seat
of the Government of the United States,
directed to the President of the Senate. The
President of the Senate shall, in the Presence
of the Senate and House of Representatives,
open all the Certificates, and the Votes
shall then be counted. The Person having
the greatest Number of Votes shall be the

President, if such Number be a Majority of the whole Number of Electors appointed; and if there be more than one who have such Majority, and have an equal Number of Votes, then the House of Representatives shall immediately chuse by Ballot one of them for President; and if no Person have a Majority, then from the five highest on the List the said House shall in like Manner chuse the President. But in chusing the President, the Votes shall be taken by States, the Representation from each State having one Vote; A quorum for this Purpose shall consist of a Member or Members from two thirds of the States, and a Majority of all the States shall be necessary to a Choice. In every Case, after the Choice of the President, the Person having the greatest Number of Votes of the Electors shall be the Vice President. But if there should remain two or more who have equal Votes, the Senate shall chuse from them by Ballot the Vice President.

The Congress may determine the Time of chusing the Electors, and the Day on which they shall give their Votes; which Day shall be the same throughout the United States.

No Person except a natural born Citizen, or a Citizen of the United States, at the time of the Adoption of this Constitution, shall be eligible to the Office of President; neither shall any Person be eligible to that Office who shall not have attained to the Age of thirty five Years, and been fourteen Years a Resident within the United States.

In Case of the Removal of the President from Office, or of his Death, Resignation, or Inability to discharge the Powers and Duties of the said Office, the Same shall devolve on the Vice President, and the Congress may by Law provide for the Case of Removal, Death, Resignation or Inability, both of the President and Vice President, declaring what Officer shall then act as President, and such Officer shall act accordingly, until the Disability be removed, or a President shall be elected.

The President shall, at stated Times, receive for his Services, a Compensation, which shall neither be encreased nor diminished during the Period for which he shall have been elected, and he shall not receive within that Period any other Emolument from the United States, or any of them.

Before he enter on the Execution of his Office, he shall take the following Oath or Affirmation:—"I do solemnly swear (or affirm) that I will faithfully execute the Office of President of the United States, and will to the best of my Ability, preserve, protect and defend the Constitution of the United States."

Section. 2.

The President shall be Commander in Chief of the Army and Navy of the United States, and of the Militia of the several States, when called into the actual Service of the United States; he may require the Opinion, in writing, of the principal Officer in each of the executive Departments, upon any Subject relating to the Duties of their respective Offices, and he shall have Power to grant Reprieves and Pardons for Offences against the United States, except in Cases of Impeachment.

He shall have Power, by and with the Advice and Consent of the Senate, to make Treaties, provided two thirds of the Senators present concur; and he shall nominate, and by and with the Advice and Consent of the Senate, shall appoint Ambassadors, other public Ministers and Consuls, Judges of the supreme Court, and all other Officers of the United States, whose Appointments are not herein otherwise provided for, and which shall be established by Law: but the Congress may by Law vest the Appointment of such inferior Officers, as they think proper, in the President alone, in the Courts of Law, or in the Heads of Departments.

The President shall have Power to fill up all Vacancies that may happen during the Recess of the Senate, by granting Commissions which shall expire at the End of their next Session.

Section. 3.

He shall from time to time give to the Congress Information of the State of the Union, and recommend to their Consideration such Measures as he shall judge necessary and expedient; he may, on extraordinary Occasions, convene both Houses, or either of them, and in Case of Disagreement between them, with Respect to the Time of Adjournment, he may adjourn them to such Time as he shall think proper; he shall receive Ambassadors and other public Ministers; he shall take Care that the Laws be faithfully executed, and shall Commission all the Officers of the United States.

Section. 4.

The President, Vice President and all civil Officers of the United States, shall be removed from Office on Impeachment for, and Conviction of, Treason, Bribery, or other high Crimes and Misdemeanors.

Article. III.

Section. 1.

The judicial Power of the United States, shall be vested in one supreme Court, and in such inferior Courts as the Congress may from time to time ordain and establish. The Judges, both of the supreme and inferior Courts, shall hold their Offices during good Behaviour, and shall, at stated Times, receive for their Services, a Compensation, which shall not be diminished during their Continuance in Office.

Section 2.

The judicial Power shall extend to all Cases, in Law and Equity, arising under this Constitution, the Laws of the United States, and Treaties made, or which shall be made, under their Authority;—to all Cases affecting Ambassadors, other public Ministers and Consuls;—to all Cases of admiralty and maritime Jurisdiction;—to Controversies to which the United States shall be a Party;—to Controversies between two or more States;— between a State and Citizens of another State,—between Citizens of different States,—between Citizens of the same State claiming Lands under Grants of different States, and between a State, or the Citizens thereof, and foreign States, Citizens or Subjects.

In all Cases affecting Ambassadors, other public Ministers and Consuls, and those in which a State shall be Party, the supreme Court shall have original Jurisdiction. In all the other Cases before mentioned, the supreme Court shall have appellate Jurisdiction, both as to Law and Fact, with such Exceptions, and under such Regulations as the Congress shall make.

The Trial of all Crimes, except in Cases of Impeachment, shall be by Jury; and such Trial shall be held in the State where the said Crimes shall have been committed; but when not committed within any State, the Trial shall be at such Place or Places as the Congress may by Law have directed.

Section. 3.

Treason against the United States, shall consist only in levying War against them, or in adhering to their Enemies, giving them Aid and Comfort. No Person shall be convicted of Treason unless on the Testimony of two Witnesses to the same overt Act, or on Confession in open Court.

The Congress shall have Power to declare the Punishment of Treason, but no Attainder of Treason shall work Corruption of Blood, or Forfeiture except during the Life of the Person attainted.

Article. IV.

Section. 1.

Full Faith and Credit shall be given in each State to the public Acts, Records, and judicial Proceedings of every other State. And the Congress may by general Laws prescribe the Manner in which such Acts, Records and Proceedings shall be proved, and the Effect thereof.

Section. 2.

The Citizens of each State shall be entitled to all Privileges and Immunities of Citizens in the several States.

A Person charged in any State with Treason, Felony, or other Crime, who shall flee from Justice, and be found in another State, shall on Demand of the executive Authority of the State from which he fled, be delivered up, to be removed to the State having Jurisdiction of the Crime.

No Person held to Service or Labour in one State, under the Laws thereof, escaping into another, shall, in Consequence of any Law or Regulation therein, be discharged from such Service or Labour, but shall be delivered up on Claim of the Party to whom such Service or Labour may be due.

Section 3.

New States may be admitted by the Congress into this Union; but no new State shall be formed or erected within the Jurisdiction of any other State; nor any State be formed by the Junction of two or more States, or Parts of States, without the Consent of the Legislatures of the States concerned as well as of the Congress.

The Congress shall have Power to dispose of and make all needful Rules and Regulations respecting the Territory or other Property belonging to the United States; and nothing in this Constitution shall be so construed as to Prejudice any Claims of the United States, or of any particular State.

Section. 4.

The United States shall guarantee to every State in this Union a Republican Form of Government, and shall protect each of them against Invasion; and on Application of the Legislature, or of the Executive (when the Legislature cannot be convened), against domestic Violence.

Article. V.

The Congress, whenever two thirds of both Houses shall deem it necessary, shall propose Amendments to this Constitution, or, on the Application of the Legislatures of two thirds of the several States, shall call a Convention for proposing Amendments, which, in either Case, shall be valid to all Intents and Purposes, as Part of this Constitution, when ratified by the Legislatures of three fourths of the several States, or by Conventions in three fourths thereof, as the one or the other Mode of Ratification may be proposed by the Congress; Provided that no Amendment which may be made prior to the Year One thousand eight hundred and eight shall in any Manner affect the first and fourth Clauses in the Ninth Section of the first Article; and that no State, without its Consent, shall be deprived of its equal Suffrage in the Senate.

 **VI.**

All Debts contracted and Engagements
entered into, before the Adoption of
this Constitution, shall be as valid
against the United States under this
Constitution, as under the Confederation.

This Constitution, and the Laws of the
United States which shall be made in
Pursuance thereof; and all Treaties made,
or which shall be made, under the Authority
of the United States, shall be the supreme
Law of the Land; and the Judges in every
State shall be bound thereby, any Thing
in the Constitution or Laws of any State
to the Contrary notwithstanding.

The Senators and Representatives before
mentioned, and the Members of the several
State Legislatures, and all executive and
judicial Officers, both of the United States
and of the several States, shall be bound
by Oath or Affirmation, to support this
Constitution; but no religious Test shall
ever be required as a Qualification to
any Office or public Trust under the
United States.

 Article. VII.

The Ratification of the Conventions of nine States, shall be sufficient for the Establishment of this Constitution between the States so ratifying the Same.

The Word, "the," being interlined between the seventh and eighth Lines of the first Page, The Word "Thirty" being partly written on an Erazure in the fifteenth Line of the first Page, The Words "is tried" being interlined between the thirty second and thirty third Lines of the first Page and the Word "the" being interlined between the forty third and forty fourth Lines of the second Page.

Done in Convention by the Unanimous Consent of the States present the Seventeenth Day of September in the Year of our Lord one thousand seven hundred and Eighty seven and of the Independance of the United States of America the Twelfth In witness whereof We have hereunto subscribed our Names,

George Washington
President and deputy from Virginia

Delaware
George Read
Gunning Bedford Jr.
John Dickinson
Richard Bassett
Jacob Broom

Maryland
James McHenry
Daniel of
    St. Thomas Jenifer
Daniel Carroll

Virginia
John Blair
James Madison Jr.

North Carolina
William Blount
Richard D. Spaight
Hugh Williamson

South Carolina
John Rutledge
Charles C. Pinckney
Pierce Butler

Georgia
William Few
Abraham Baldwin

New Hampshire
John Langdon
Nicholas Gilman

Massachusetts
Nathaniel Gorham
Rufus King

Connecticut
William S. Johnson
Roger Sherman

New York
Alexander Hamilton

New Jersey
William Livingston
David Brearley
William Paterson
Jonathan Dayton

Pensylvania
Benjamin Franklin
Thomas Mifflin
Robert Morris
George Clymer
Thomas FitzSimons
Jared Ingersoll
James Wilson
Gouverneur Morris

Bill of Rights

The Bill of Rights is the first 10 Amendments to the Constitution. They were written by James Madison, and approved by Congress on September 25, 1789. After the Congress agreed to the amendments, three-fourths of the states (11 states out of 14 at the time) ratified them about two years later on December 15, 1791. Secretary of State Thomas Jefferson certified their adoption on March 1, 1792.

Since this time 17 additional amendments have been approved by the Congress and ratified by three-fourths of the states.

Amendment the 1st

Congress shall make no law respecting an establishment of religion, or prohibiting the free exercise thereof; or abridging the freedom of speech; or of the press; or the right of the people to peaceably assemble, and to petition the Government for a redress of grievances.

Amendment the 2d

A well-regulated Militia, being necessary to the security of a free State, the right of the people to keep and bear Arms, shall not be infringed.

Amendment the 3d
No soldier shall, in time of peace, be quartered in any house without the consent of the owner, nor in time of war, but in a manner to be prescribed by law.

Amendment the 4th
The right of the People to be secure in their persons, houses, papers and effects, against unreasonable searches and seizures, shall not be violated, and no warrants shall issue, but upon probable cause supported by oath or affirmation, and particularly describing the place to be searched, and the person or things to be seized.

Amendment the 5th
No person shall be held to answer for a capital, or otherwise infamous crime, unless on a presentment or indictment of a Grand Jury, except in cases arising in the land or naval forces, or in the Militia, when in actual service in time of War or public danger, nor shall any person be subject for the same offense to be twice put in jeopardy of life or limb, nor shall be compelled in any criminal case to be a witness against himself, nor be deprived of life, liberty, or property, without due process of law, nor shall private property be taken for public use, without just compensation.

Amendment the 6th
In all criminal prosecutions, the accused shall enjoy the right to a speedy and public

trial by an impartial jury of the State and district wherein the crime shall have been committed, which district shall have been previously ascertained by law, and to be informed of the nature and cause of the accusation, to be confronted with the witnesses against him, to have compulsory process for obtaining witnesses in his favor, and to have the Assistance of Counsel for his defense.

Amendment the 7th

In suits at common law, where the value in controversy shall exceed twenty dollars, the right of trial by Jury shall be preserved, and no fact, tried by a Jury, shall be otherwise re-examined in any court of the United States, than according to the rules of the common law.

Amendment the 8th

Excessive bail shall not be required, nor excessive fines imposed, nor cruel and unusual punishments inflicted.

Amendment the 9th

The enumeration in the Constitution, of certain rights, shall not be construed to deny or disparage others retained by the people.

Amendment the 10th

The powers not delegated by the Constitution, nor prohibited by it to the States, are reserved to the States respectively, or to the people.

Made in the USA
Middletown, DE
17 December 2017